Muffin
& THE LESSON OF KOKUA

Written and Illustrated by Carmen Geshell
Illustrations painted by Janice Nantkes

Produced, published and distributed by
Island Heritage Publishing

ISBN Number 0-89610-289-0
First Edition, First Printing 1995

 Address orders and editorial correspondence to:
ISLAND HERITAGE PUBLISHING
A division of The Madden Corporation
99-880 Iwaena Street
Telephone (808) 487-7299

Muffin

& THE LESSON OF KOKUA

Cast of Characters

Reggae Muff

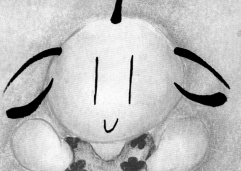

Muffin

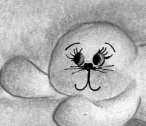

Auntie Pueo

Wili

Milli

Fingers

Keoki

This book is dedicated
in loving memory
of my Tutu Mimi.
Special thanks
to my mother :
Mom, you are the best!

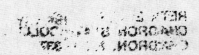

Muffin

& THE LESSON OF KOKUA

Written & Illustrated
by Carmen Geshell

Illustrations Painted
by Janice Nantkes

An Island Heritage Book

There is a very special dog with wild hair and a big heart who lives on the island of Oʻahu in the chain of Hawaiian Islands.

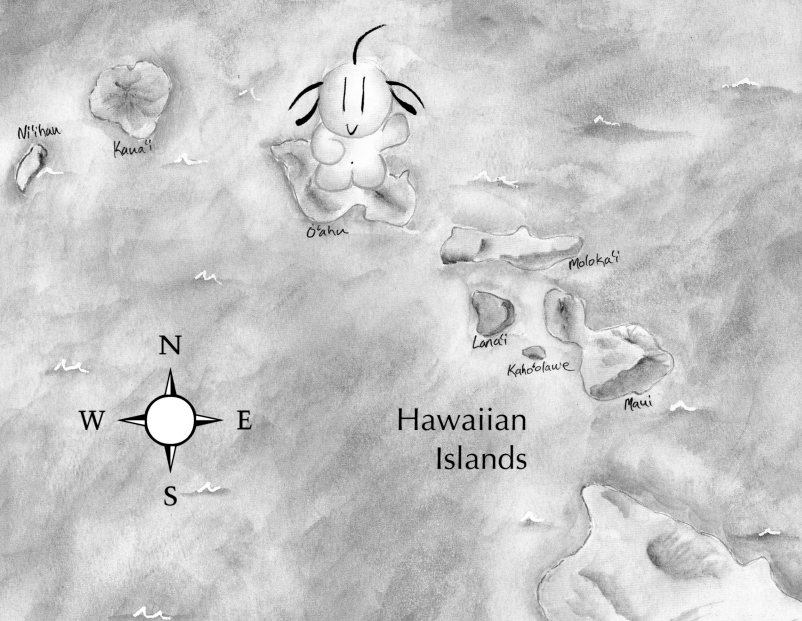

Niʻihau

Kauaʻi

Oʻahu

Molokaʻi

Lanaʻi

Kahoʻolawe

Maui

Hawaiian
Islands

Pacific Ocean

Hawaiʻi
(The Big Island)

Her name is Muffin, and she is the Canine Ambassador of the Aloha Spirit, which is a very important job. Muffin earned the title because of her great love of the Islands and everyone and everything in them.

One day, Muffin's best friend, Reggae Muff, came for a visit.
It had been a long plane ride from his home in Jamaica — clear
across two oceans! — and Reggae Muff was happy to be in
Hawai'i with his friend.

Muffin greeted him with a *lei* and a welcoming *Aloha*.

"*Aloha, Mon!*" replied Reggae Muff. "I know what that means—hello, good-bye and love."

"I see you've been studying Hawaiian," commented Muffin.

"Ya, *Mon*, I want to speak with the best of them. Will you teach me some more Hawaiian?" he asked.

"No problem, *Mon!*" smiled Muffin.

Reggae Muff smiled, too. Muffin had been studying the Jamaican way of speaking as well.

"What is the first thing
you want to do?" asked Muffin
as they looked through stacks
of guidebooks and maps.

9

"Go surfing!" exclaimed Reggae Muff with much anticipation. In his homeland of Jamaica, Reggae Muff is a famous surfer, known to many as the *Irie* Pup. It had been a dream of his to surf the big waves of O'ahu's famous North Shore.

"All right, let's go! The waves are perfect up at Sunset and Waimea. We had a big storm the other night, so the waves ought to be a nice size."

The two headed off to the North Shore with their surfboards. Along the way, Muffin pointed out various points of interest and translated some Hawaiian words.

— Da Kine Menu —
Shave Ice   Musubi
Plate Lunch   Fruit Punch
Malasada   Soda

BENTO

After stopping for
shave ice (a local treat that
Muffin had to introduce to Reggae
Muff), the two made their way to one
of the famous surfing beaches for which the
North Shore is known.

"When we were at the airport, I kept hearing the
word *kokua*. What does it mean?" asked Reggae Muff
as they walked down to the water's edge.

"Oh, that's an easy one," replied Muffin
in-between the last bits of her shave ice. "It means—"

"LOOK!" shouted Reggae Muff, as he pointed to a figure lying on the beach. Upon further investigation, they found that it was a baby Hawaiian monk seal.

"Where's your mommy, little guy?" asked Muffin
as she bent down to talk with the seal.

The little seal's eyes began to well up and soon over
flowed with tears. Muffin looked at Reggae Muff, who shrugged.

"What's the trouble, *Mon?*" asked Reggae Muff, trying
to be helpful.

"The name's Wili," said the seal in-between sobs.
"And I can't find her."

"Your mommy?" repeated Muffin.

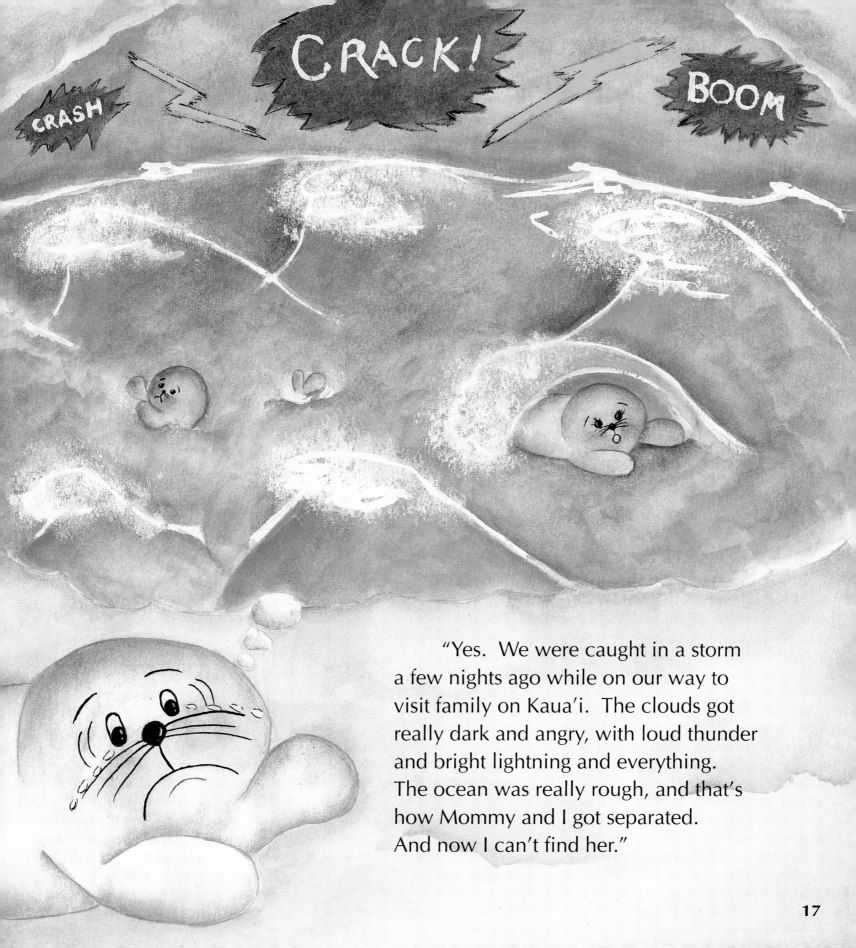

"Yes. We were caught in a storm a few nights ago while on our way to visit family on Kaua'i. The clouds got really dark and angry, with loud thunder and bright lightning and everything. The ocean was really rough, and that's how Mommy and I got separated. And now I can't find her."

17

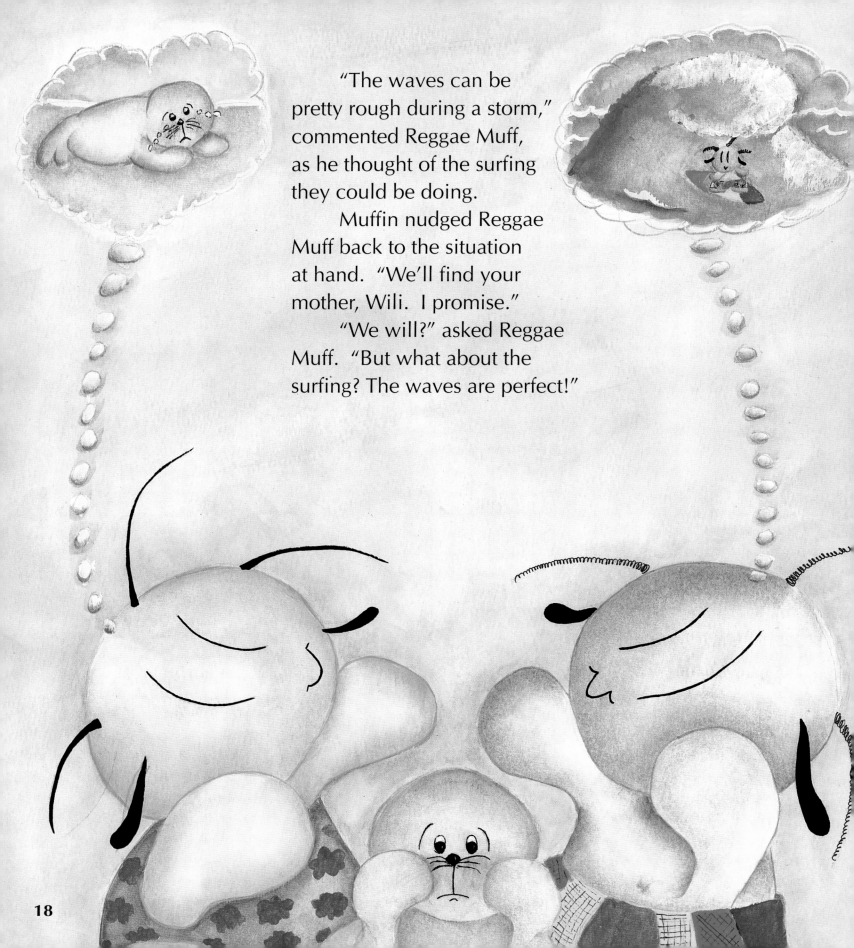

"The waves can be pretty rough during a storm," commented Reggae Muff, as he thought of the surfing they could be doing.

Muffin nudged Reggae Muff back to the situation at hand. "We'll find your mother, Wili. I promise."

"We will?" asked Reggae Muff. "But what about the surfing? The waves are perfect!"

"They can wait!" said Muffin as she grabbed Reggae
Muff's arm. "We've got places to go and people to talk to.
Don't worry, Wili—we'll have your mommy back by
sundown tonight," Muffin called out to the baby seal
as they left the beach.

Reggae Muff hoped she was right, and so did Muffin.
They had to be!

Muffin and Reggae Muff journeyed into the forest in search of Auntie Pueo, who is the wisest owl in all of *Hawai'i Nei*. If anyone would know what to do and how to go about it, Auntie would know.

"Are you sure about this, Muffin?" asked Reggae Muff as he stepped over a fallen tree branch.

"Sure I'm sure. Auntie is the one to ask."

"I still think that the Marines would be better."

"Naw, they're too busy. Besides, Auntie Pueo knows everything that's going on."

21

Just then there was a great WOOSH and the leaves and flowers of the trees shook from the great wind that was created. "Did I hear my name mentioned?" said a voice after the dust and flying leaves cleared.

"Auntie, it's you!"
exclaimed Muffin.
"And WHOOOO else?"
laughed Auntie Pueo.

"We could really use your help. My friend, Reggae Muff,
and I found a lost baby seal down on the beach."
"Yeah, and the *mon* can't find his mama," added Reggae Muff.
"Oh, that is a bit of a *pilikia*," sighed Auntie.
"That means trouble, doesn't it!"
asked Reggae Muff.
Auntie Pueo looked surprised,
but very happy, to hear
that Muffin's friend was
studying the beautiful
Hawaiian language.
"Can you tell me
what *kokua* means?"
"That's an easy one."
Auntie flapped her wing
in the air. "It means—"

23

Just then, there was another great rustling of leaves and tree branches. This time it was Keoki, the sea gull, crashing into the canopy of the forest. He looked very excited about something!

"Auntie! I'm so glad I found you! Oh, I don't know what I'll do. It's just terrible! What will we do?"

"Slow down, Keoki," said Auntie Pueo calmly. "Take things one at a time. Now, what is the problem?"

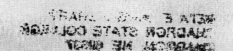

24

Keoki took a deep breath and began. "I was out catching food for my dinner tonight when I saw it."

"Saw what, Keoki?" asked Muffin.

"There was a lot of trash and seaweed and just plain junk in the water. It was terrible. You know, we really should clean it up. That's what I thought. As I was looking through the mess, a voice called out to me. I turned around and I was looking right at this poor lady seal who was all tangled up and couldn't get free."

"Wili's mother!" Muffin and Reggae Muff shouted in unison as they looked at each other.

"Well, whoever she is, we must help
that seal. Come on—I'll show you where
I found her," said Keoki breathlessly.

"Hey, wait, Keoki," Reggae Muff said to the sea gull. "Do you know
what kokua means?"

"Not now, Reggae—We don't have time to talk. We have to go save
that seal!" exclaimed Muffin.

Muffin and Reggae Muff thanked the sea gull and Auntie Pueo
as well. Auntie bid them luck
and promised to keep
her feathers crossed,
just in case.

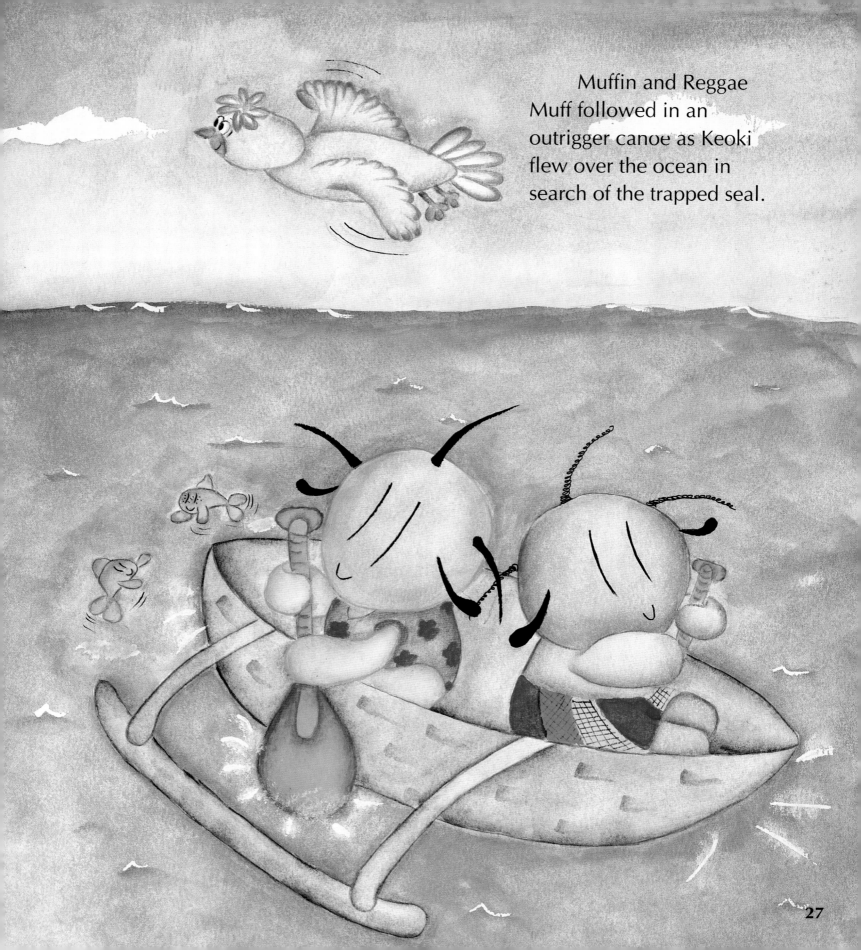

Muffin and Reggae Muff followed in an outrigger canoe as Keoki flew over the ocean in search of the trapped seal.

The trio finally found her and set about the task of untangling her.
"Is my little Wili alright?" asked Milli, the mother seal.
"Yes, he's fine. But he misses you and is very worried," replied
Muffin as she jumped into the water to help out.

"Keoki," Muffin called to the gull as he circled overhead, "Would you go tell Wili that we found his mother and not to worry!"

Keoki cawed a reply and headed back to land to relay the good news.

Reggae Muff secured the canoe with a string of seaweed and hopped in to help Muffin. The task of freeing Milli was going to be harder than they thought.

"If only we had another two hands to help out," sighed Muffin. "Yeah, all we've got is four. You and me!" agreed Reggae Muff.

"Perhaps I may be of service. I have eight!" said
a garbled voice. "My name is Fingers, and I'd be happy
to lend a hand – or two – or three – or however many!"

Muffin thanked the octopus profusely, and she and Reggae Muff got out of the way so Fingers could do his stuff. With his many arms, Fingers was able to undo Milli from the mess of litter, seaweed and junk in no time. The grateful seal thanked them all and promised to help her rescuers if they were ever in trouble.

"Maybe you can help me." Reggae Muff turned to Fingers.
"Can you tell me what kokua means?"

The octopus would have answered Reggae Muff's
question—if he could have heard it. Unfortunately, Fingers was
clapping his many arms together in celebration of Milli's rescue.

Reggae Muff shook his head, and everyone headed back
to the beach for the reunion.

When the group arrived back at the beach, they were greeted with cheers of Aloha from Keoki, Auntie Pueo and especially Wili. Milli charged up to the beach upon seeing her baby. Everyone who had helped out felt rewarded when the seals were finally reunited.

In honor of the happy occasion, Muffin decided to throw a lu'au. Everyone who helped rescue Milli was invited, and there would be plenty of fun for all.

"This is sure a great party!   I mean lu'au, Muffin," said Reggae Muff, as he tasted some poi. "But I still haven't found out what kokua means."

"Remember when we agreed to help find Wili's mom?" Muffin asked as she watched the two seals cuddling. "And how Auntie Pueo said she'd find out what to do?" Muffin noticed the owl dancing to the music that Reggae Muff brought from Jamaica. "And how Keoki and Fingers did their parts in finding and freeing Milli?"

"Yes, but what does that have to do with the word kokua?" shrugged Reggae Muff.

"In all of those times, they were helping and using cooperation. That is what kokua means," Muffin explained.

"I get it now," Reggae Muff smiled. "The answer was there all the time! Mahalo nui loa, Muffin!" he said using another Hawaiian phrase.